little Miss Naughty

by Roger Hargreaves

PSS!
PRICE STERN SLOAN
An Imprint of Penguin Group (USA) Inc.

Are you ever naughty?

Sometimes, I bet!

Well, Little Miss Naughty was naughty all the time.

She woke up one Sunday morning and looked out of the window.

"Looks like a nice day," she said to herself.

And then she grinned.

"Looks like a nice day for being naughty," she said.

And rubbed her hands!

That Sunday, Mr. Uppity was out for his morning stroll.

Little Miss Naughty knocked his hat off his head.

And jumped on it!

"My hat!" cried Mr. Uppity.

That afternoon, Mr. Clever was sitting in his garden reading a book.

And do you know what that Little Miss Naughty did?

She broke his glasses!

"My glasses!" cried Mr. Clever.

That evening, Mr. Bump was just standing there.

Minding his own business.

And guess what Little Miss Naughty did?

She ran off with his bandages!

And bandaged up Mr. Small!

"Mmmmmmmmmmmfffff!" he cried.

It's difficult to say anything when you're bandaged up like that!

Mr. Uppity and Mr. Clever and Mr. Bump and Mr. Small were very very very very cross.

Very very very very cross indeed!

"Oh what a wonderful Sunday," giggled Little Miss Naughty as she walked along. "And it isn't even bedtime yet!"

First thing on Monday morning, the Mr. Men had a meeting.

"Something has to be done," announced Mr. Uppity, who had managed to straighten out his hat.

They all looked at Mr. Clever, who was wearing his spare pair of glasses.

"You're the cleverest," they said. "What's to be done about Little Miss Naughty?"

Mr. Clever thought.

He cleared his throat.

And spoke.

"I have no idea," he said.

"I have," piped up Mr. Small.

"I know what that naughty little lady needs," he went on. "And I know who can do it," he added.

"What?" asked Mr. Uppity.

"Who?" asked Mr. Clever.

"Aha!" chuckled Mr. Small, and went off to see a friend of his.

Somebody who could do impossible things.

Somebody who could do impossible things like making himself invisible.

I wonder who that could be?

That Monday, Mr. Nosey was asleep under a tree.

Little Miss Naughty crept toward him with a pot of paint in one hand, a paintbrush in the other, and a rather large grin on her face.

She was going to paint the end of his nose!

Red!

But.

Just as she was about to do the dreadful deed, something happened.

TWEAK!

Somebody tweaked her nose!

Somebody she couldn't see tweaked her nose!

Somebody invisible!

I wonder who!

"Ouch!" cried Little Miss Naughty.

And, dropping the paint and paintbrush, she ran away as fast as her little legs would carry her.

One Tuesday, Mr. Busy was rushing along.

As usual!

Little Miss Naughty, standing by the side of the road, stuck out her foot.

She was going to trip him!

Head over heels!

And heels over head!

But.

Just before she did, something happened.

TWEAK!

The invisible nose tweaker had struck again!

And it hurt!

"Ouch!" cried Little Miss Naughty.

And ran away even faster than her little legs would carry her.

On Wednesday, Mr. Happy was at home.

Watching television!

Outside, Little Miss Naughty picked up a stone.

She was going to break his window!

Naughty girl!

But.

As she brought her arm back to throw, guess what?

That's right!

TWEAK!

"Ouch!" cried Little Miss Naughty as she ran off
holding her nose.

And so it went on.

All day Thursday.

TWEAK!

All day Friday.

TWEAK! TWEAK!

"Hello Mr. Impossible," he smiled. "Thank you for helping to cure Little Miss Naughty."

"My pleasure," laughed Mr. Impossible. "But it did take all week."

Mr. Small grinned.

"Don't you mean," he said, "all tweak?"

Biblical Foundation 3

New Testament Baptisms

by Larry Kreider

House To House Publications
Lititz, Pennsylvania USA

New Testament Baptisms

Larry Kreider

Updated Edition © 2002, Reprinted 2003, 2005
Copyright © 1993, 1997, 1999
House to House Publications
11 Toll Gate Road, Lititz, PA 17543
Telephone: 800.848.5892
Web site: www.dcfi.org

ISBN 1-886973-02-4
Design and illustrations by Sarah Sauder

Unless otherwise noted, all scripture quotations in this publication are taken from the *Holy Bible, New International Version* (NIV).
© 1973, 1978, 1984 by International Bible Society. Used by permission of Zondervan Publishing House. All rights reserved.